ARBOR HILL-WEST HILL BRANCH
ALBANY PUBLIC LIBRARY

D0254527

## Parents and Caregivers,

Stone Arch Readers are designed to provide [...]
experiences, as well as opportunities to develop vocabulary,
literacy skills, and comprehension. Here are a few ways to
support your beginning reader:

- Talk with your child about the ideas addressed in the story.

- Discuss each illustration, mentioning the characters, where they
  are, and what they are doing.

- Read with expression, pointing to each word. You may want to
  read the whole story through and then revisit parts of the story to
  ensure that the meanings of words or phrases are understood.

- Talk about why the character did what he or she did and what
  your child would do in that situation.

- Help your child connect with characters and events in the story.

Remember, reading with your child should be fun, not forced. Each
moment spent reading with your child is a priceless investment in
his or her literacy life.

**Gail Saunders-Smith, Ph.D**

# STONE ARCH **READERS**

are published by Stone Arch Books
151 Good Counsel Drive, P.O. Box 669
Mankato, Minnesota 56002
www.stonearchbooks.com

Copyright © 2010 by Stone Arch Books

All rights reserved. No part of this publication may be reproduced
in whole or in part, or stored in a retrieval system, or transmitted in any
form or by any means, electronic, mechanical, photocopying, recording,
or otherwise, without written permission of the publisher.

Library of Congress Cataloging-in-Publication Data
Suen, Anastasia.
   Skate trick : a Robot and Rico story / by Anastasia Suen ; illustrated by
Mike Laughead.
   p. cm. – (Stone Arch readers)
   ISBN 978-1-4342-1629-8 (library binding)
   ISBN 978-1-4342-1750-9 (pbk.)
   [1. Skateboarding–Fiction. 2. Robots–Fiction.] I. Laughead, Mike, ill. II. Title.
PZ7.S94343Sk 2010
[E]–dc22

                                                            2009000885

Summary: Rico knows lots of tricks on his skateboard. Robot wants to learn too.
Find out if Robot can master the skateboard or if he ends up crashing.

Art Director: Bob Lentz
Graphic Designer: Hilary Wacholz

Reading Consultants:
Gail Saunders-Smith, Ph.D
Melinda Melton Crow, M.Ed
Laurie K. Holland, Media Specialist

Printed in the United States of America

# SKATE TRICK

## A ROBOT AND RICO STORY

BY ANASTASIA SUEN
ILLUSTRATED BY MIKE LAUGHEAD

STONE ARCH BOOKS
MINNEAPOLIS   SAN DIEGO

This is ROBOT.
Robot has lots of
tools. He uses the
tools to help his
best friend, **Rico**.

Teapot

Wings

Scissors

Fire Finger

Special Shoes

Roller Skates

Rico rolls on his board.
Pop! Jump!

"Watch my new skateboard trick," says Rico.

"Can I try?" asks Robot.

"Sure," says Rico. He gives the skateboard to Robot.

Robot stands on the skateboard.

"What do I do?" he asks.

"Roll," says Rico.

"I can do that," says Robot.

"Now jump," says Rico.

"I can do that," says Robot.

Crash! Robot lands in a tree.

"Are you okay?" asks Rico.

"I'm sad," says Robot.

"Don't be sad," says Rico. "It takes time to learn a new trick."

"It does?" asks Robot. "Can I try again?"

"Sure," says Rico.

Robot stands on the skateboard.

"What do I do?" he asks.

"Roll," says Rico. "Now jump."

Crash! Robot falls on the ground.

"Are you okay?" asks Rico.

"I cannot do it," says Robot.

"It takes time to learn a new trick," says Rico.

"I see," says Robot.

"Let's fix you. Then you can try again," says Rico.

Robot stands on the skateboard.

"Roll," says Rico.

"Now what?" asks Robot.

"Jump on the rail," says Rico.

Crack! The skateboard breaks
in half.

"Oh no!" says Rico.

"Don't be sad," says Robot.
"I can make you a new one."

"I can make two," says Robot.
"One for you and one for me."

Robot gets to work.

Robot gives Rico the new skateboard.

"Thanks!" says Rico.

"Now it is my turn," says Robot.
"Watch this trick."

Zoom! Roll! Jump! Robot does a
great new trick.

"You did it!" yells Rico.

"Let's do it again!" says Robot.

# STORY WORDS

roll          skateboard     crash

jump         trick

Total Word Count: 277

**One robot. One boy. One crazy fun friendship! Read all four Robot and Rico adventures!**